THE PARABLE OF THE SOWER

That same day Jesus left the house and went to the lakeside, where he sat down to teach. The crowd gathered around him was so large that he got into a boat and sat in it, while the crowd stood on the shore. He used parables to tell them many things.

"There was a man who went out to sow. As he scattered the seed in the field, some of it fell along the path, and the birds came and ate it up. Some of it fell on rocky ground, where there was little soil. The seeds soon sprouted, because the soil wasn't deep. When the sun came up it burned the young plants, and because the roots had not grown deep enough the plants soon dried up. Some of the seed fell among thorns, which grew up and choked the plants. But some seeds fell in good soil, and bore grain: some had one hundred grains, others sixty, and others thirty." And Jesus said, "Listen, then, if you have ears!" St Matthew 13, 1-9

Acknowledgment

The above quotation from The Good News Bible *is reproduced by permission of Collins Publishers.*

The parable of
THE SOWER

retold for easy reading
by SYLVIA MANDEVILLE

illustrated by DAVID PALMER

Ladybird Books Loughborough

THE SOWER

The summer is over now, the harvest is finished, and the ground is ready to be planted with new corn.

Today, I went up to one of my big fields, which looks over Lake Galilee. While I was there, something happened which made me think.

Let me tell you about it.

5

I set off early from home, before the sun got hot. My wife had the big basket ready, full of the best grain, saved from the summer harvest. My little girl Rebecca handed me some food she had prepared, a few small loaves and some dried figs.

Then I was off for the day! The field I am telling you about has a footpath running through it and people often walk along it from Capernaum to our village.

The field gently slopes, and although some soil is good, there are large rocky patches which are not much use.

At one end of the field is a very difficult patch. Thorn bushes and weeds keep on growing there.

When I got to the field I set to work, sowing corn. Carrying my basket of seed, I walked up and down the field taking handfuls of grain from the basket and flinging it over the ground.

As the day wore on and I walked up and down, up and down, scattering my seed, I noticed that down below on the edge of Lake Galilee, a crowd was gathering.

Friends and neighbours were hurrying through my field down to the lake. "We are going to see Jesus," one of them said. "He is spending the day by the lake. Why don't you come?"

Now, I had heard about Jesus from many people. Our friend's little girl had been very ill and Jesus had healed her. A real miracle.

We had all talked and talked about that. Also, one of my nephews, a fisherman, is always telling me about Him. He is sure that everything that Jesus says is true.

13

So when my neighbour asked me to go down to the lake for the day, I was very tempted.

I wanted to see Jesus for myself. Then I thought of my crop which had to be planted. If I didn't plant the corn, what should we have to eat next year?

No, I decided, a poor farmer like me can't take a day off just when he likes.

Rather sadly, I carried on with my work, walking up and down, up and down, sowing the seed.

When I sat down under an olive tree to eat my lunch, I saw there was a large crowd down by the lake. I could see

Jesus, sitting in a boat at the water's edge, so that everyone could see and hear Him.

After lunch, I went on with my work, and forgot all about them. By evening I had covered over half the field.

I plodded slowly home, quite tired. As I got near to my house, Rebecca ran out to meet me.

Her face was alight with excitement. My wife looked happy too. "Rebecca has something to tell you," she said. "She has been down by the lake all day with her friends, listening to Jesus. She has only just got back."

"Listening to Jesus?" I said. "Well, you are a lucky girl. I wanted to leave my work and go down to listen myself."

"Oh, but it is good that you didn't," said Rebecca, "because then Jesus would not have been able to tell us one of His stories. Do you know, we could all see you up on the field, walking up and down, up and down, sowing your grain, and Jesus told us a story about YOU!"

21

"A story about me?" I exclaimed. "What did He say?"

"Well, He said that one day there was a farmer who went out to sow corn. As he scattered the seed, up and down the field, some of the corn fell

onto the path, and not only
did the birds come and eat it
up, but passers-by trod on it,
and no seed grew."

Rebecca jumped up and
down with excitement as she
told me the story.

"Jesus said next that some of the seed fell onto rocky ground, where the soil was very shallow. The seeds there soon sprouted, but the hot sun burned the young plants because they could not send down roots deep enough to find water."

"Oh, I've seen that happen year after year up on our fields," I told Rebecca. "There are great patches of rocky ground, with only very shallow soil. The plants shoot up, and then wither. We never get a crop off that soil.

"What did He say next?"

2

"Let me think," said Rebecca. "Yes, I remember. He said that as the farmer went up and down the field, some of his grain fell among patches of thorns and weeds.

"That corn sprouted well in the moist earth, and took root and grew quite tall, but the weeds grew thicker and faster and choked the tender seedlings. They never did produce any grain."

"Just what I was thinking myself, today," I said. "You know those thorns and weeds, don't you, Rebecca, at the top of that field? However much I try to root them out, they still grow again. The corn never thrives there. As Jesus said, the corn shoots up and then it gets choked. Is that the end of the story?"

"No, there was a bit more. Jesus said that as the farmer strode across the field, some of the corn fell on good rich soil, and the plants sprouted, took root deep into the ground and grew up tall and strong.

"Slowly and gradually they produced ears of corn which ripened in the sun.

"Some produced thirty grains, some produced sixty grains, and some produced a hundred grains."

"Yes, that's true," I said. "Of course there are never enough plants which produce a hundred grains. That is very rare. There's nothing I enjoy

more than standing looking at
a field of ripe corn, with all
the ears full of grain.

"Did Jesus say anything else?"

"Yes, He said that if we have ears, we must listen to the story," said Rebecca.

"But I've got ears, and I have listened to the story, and I don't understand what it means."

She looked at her mother.

"I don't know either," said my wife, "but it must mean more than just telling us a story about planting corn."

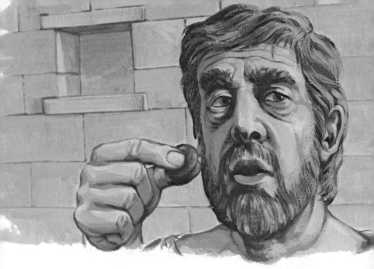

I did not say much during supper. I was thinking about the story and wondering what it meant.

I also had a plan — after supper I would call on my nephew the fisherman, and find out what he thought about the story.

When it was quite dark I left our house and went down to him. He had not gone out on his night fishing and was pleased to talk.

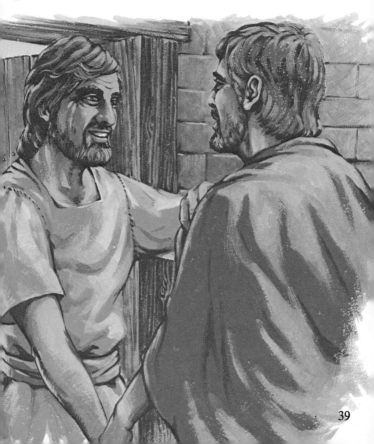

"My Rebecca has been telling me the story of the sower that Jesus told today. Well, of course, it is very true what He said, in fact He must know my field like the back of His hand, but what does it mean? I couldn't work it out."

"We were puzzled too," my nephew said. "Later on when the crowd had gone, we asked Jesus about it. He was surprised that we did not understand it. This is how He explained it."

The young fisherman thought for a moment. "The seed which the sower scatters is the word of God – the message God has to tell us.

"The seeds that fell along the path, where the birds ate them, are like people who hear God's message, but before they can understand it and let it take root in their minds, the devil comes and takes the message away. Then they can no longer believe and trust in God."

My nephew went on, "The seeds that fell on rocky ground stand for all the people who hear about God and believe in Him very quickly.

"They are glad to hear about God, but the message does not sink down deep into them. They believe in God only for a little while. When things go wrong and people are angry with them for trusting God, they give up and do not believe any more.

"Jesus said next that the seeds that fell in among the thorns, stand for people who hear about God and believe in Him, and want to serve Him. They have got so many worries, and

so much money, and they are so busy trying to have a good time, that they have no time left for God Himself. Their faith gets choked by all these other things.

"The seeds that fell into the good soil are like the people who hear about God, and keep His message firmly in their hearts, and do what he says.

"They grow steadily. Gradually they bear God's fruit in their lives. Some bear a little, some a bit more, and some a great deal."

"I'd like to be that sort of person," I said, "but what is the fruit that God wants us to bear?"

My nephew said, "I think it means that when God's message has taken root in our lives, it gradually changes us. We become the sort of people God wants us to be."

"Do you mean kinder, and wanting to share more, and being forgiving?" I asked.

"Yes, and being truthful, and doing what God wants us to do all through our lives."

"I shall have plenty to think about tomorrow," I said.